BELL-EYE, THE BEST, LITTLEST DETECTIVE AGENCY IN PALM BEACH, FLORIDA

BELL-EYE, THE BEST, LITTLEST DETECTIVE AGENCY IN PALM BEACH, FLORIDA

The Lives of The Rich, Famous and Naughty

BARRETT K. HAYS M.D., INDIA HAYS, AND BELLA

authorHOUSE®

AuthorHouse™
1663 Liberty Drive
Bloomington, IN 47403
www.authorhouse.com
Phone: 1-800-839-8640

Published by AuthorHouse   10/16/2012

ISBN: 978-1-4772-7158-2 (sc)
ISBN: 978-1-4772-7156-8 (e)

Library of Congress Control Number: 2012917453

Any people depicted in stock imagery provided by Thinkstock are models, and such images are being used for illustrative purposes only. Certain stock imagery © Thinkstock.

This book is printed on acid-free paper.

THAT CERTAIN RING BELL-EYE

Hello, my name is Bella. I run a detective agency in Palm Beach, Florida. I have only one client—the fabulously rich heiress, India Hays. Yes, *that* India Hays. Only one client, you say? Well, India is very particular and she would not approve of me working another job. She doesn't know that I own and run the smallest and smartest detective agency in Palm Beach. My agency is called Bell-eye. I am Bell-eye. I have one assistant, a Daschund named Winston, an incurable romantic who is easily befuddled and bemused. Good help is hard to find, even in Palm Beach.

You would like Palm Beach. The weather is good most of the year. The crime rate is low. But even I must admit, crime attempts are not.

Palm Beach is an affluent community. Most of our residents have business interests that usually bring an individual at least one million dollars a year. We aren't talking principle or total assets, I am simply saying millionaires are a dime a dozen here. India Hays's dad is a billionaire. I couldn't tell you her net worth, or could I? Client confidentiality! Palm Beach is home to the working rich and the idle rich. India is the working rich. Her dad is always expecting her to have a new idea, a new deal going. And this is where I come in. I have been engaged by my client to see that she doesn't get fleeced, hurt, or taken by anyone. She has lawyers, two bodyguards, and the Palm Beach Police on her side. And she has me, a three-pound Chihuahua. By the way, I was the one who first engaged my services. I have perks, so an income isn't necessary. Excuse me, Perrier Water please with a twist of lime. I will take the two ounce filet mignon, rare. Thank you. A girl has to watch her figure. Sorry, I had to place an order with our chef, Rene. He's from France and he is really good. Honestly, *il est tres chic*. But I digress. Now where was I? Ah yes. India, for example, didn't know Molly Sherbin. Molly blew into town with impeccable references. She had gone to Radcliffe. She was in the Social Register. And she was even in

Town and Country. On the surface, she seemed okay.

But my ears perked up when she wanted a mere two million dollars for a boys' shelter in West Palm Beach. It was such a trifle, pocket change for her cause. Her brochures were fabulous. Her hair was perfect. Her jewelry was magnificent. Her shoes were so Jimmy Achew. I sneezed. Well, India is going shopping on Worth Avenue. Her chauffeur, Marcus, and two bodyguards are going with her. That's Gino and DiMarco. Mean hombres if you catch my drift. But otherwise, her posse is rather nice. India is buying a dress, a pair of shoes, a piece of jewelry, eyewear, and matching accessories for her favorite dog—me!

We have a night to celebrate. I will be wearing Marc Jacobs's "Daisy." That's my favorite scent. I wear Red L'Oreal lipstick. India will be wearing a Prada dress, Fendi shoes, a Tiffany bracelet, and a Harry Winston pair of eight-carat diamond earrings. I love her style. I am not bragging, but even an heiress has to keep an inventory. I even have a jeweler's loupe. Believe me, in Palm Beach, one should carry around her jeweler's loupe like a driver's license.

I like driving down Worth Avenue. The car, a Bentley of course, becomes crowded though.

India also owns a Mercedes Landau with fully reclinable rear seats. But we have to deal with Gino, DiMarco, and Marcus. I call them the three goons, but not to their faces. Sometimes I think our staff is too big. Three guys all the time. There is also Rene the chef, Larry and Lucy are the housekeepers, and Mr. Barnes, the horticulturist who supervises the landscapers and our greenhouse. Of course, don't forget her personal trainer, her accountant, her lawyers, her personal secretary, and her physician. There is also the pilot. Thank God she doesn't have a hairdresser on staff. Can you imagine the payroll, plus expenses? But we don't live in Palm Beach year-round. It's only for the season. And then it's off to New York and traveling. We live on the Park, and it's rather nice, though crowded. When we are there, we only have Gino, Rene, Lucy, and Marcus.

I am in the car now and we're driving down Worth Avenue. Oh no, guess who I see? It's Molly Sherbin. She has on Jimmy Choo shoes, a Chanel dress, and a Louis Vuitton bag. Her diamonds are magnificent. Maybe the Sherbins still have moola. India instructs Marcus to stop the car and off we go. We are shopping with Molly Sherbin today and eating lunch at LeReve. It's a quiet party for donors. If you are truly rich, you have to give money away. If you can give the money away, then you possess your riches; if you can't, then your riches possess you. Let's see if I can eavesdrop.

"Molly, I love your jewelry, especially your ring!"

"Oh, this one? It's my shopping ring. It belonged to my Grandmother."

"How very nice. How many people are coming to our fete?"

"Perhaps ten. That's only twenty million dollars. I was hoping to raise thirty million."

"Molly, you worry too much. You will see that people are very nice and quite generous."

Did you hear that? The ring belonged to her grandmother. I am no jeweler, but I don't think that the style or cut of the stones was popular in her grandmother's day. And for her to say that's only twenty million dollars. Something doesn't sound right! Well, maybe I am being too judgmental.

The weather is always beautiful in Palm Beach. I am going outside now to lap pool water and chat with my neighbor, Winston Beaumont III. Yes, that same Beaumont. The Beaumont Hotels are legendary. Winston, as I mentioned before, is also my assistant. No, he doesn't need the money. In fact, there has never been money exchanged at my agency, just gratitude. About two weeks ago, I brought the studious

Mr. Beaumont a book on languages. I hope that has given him something to do with his time since the Beaumonts don't need more money.

"Hi, Bella. I want to thank you for my book. I never realized that there were so many languages!"

He's no Sherlock, but he plays a pretty decent Watson. "Hi, Winston! Don't step on those flowers. Mr. Barnes is a terror."

"I can translate languages other than English with this book."

"So you can! And?"

"Well, I found this note in Thai."

"Let me see that note. It has a ring on it. I don't read Thai, Winston."

"I don't either, but an English translation is on the back."

"Bancock Gemstones. Sent to Sharon Jones, 1066 Dimwhip, Apt. A, West Palm Beach, Florida. One setting. Eight zirconia, one carat each, and one yellow simulated diamond. Total: 80 US dollars. Well, I smell a rat!"

"Where? Here?"

"No, you dolt! That's the ring Molly Sherbin said belonged to her Grandmother. It probably did yesterday. Let's get a telephone number in the reverse listing phonebook. Come with me. We will use the pool house phone."

"Here's the number for Sharon Jones."

"It's ringing!"

"Hello?"

"Yes, this is Palm Beach Orchids. We were given this address for Molly Sherbin. Can we make our free delivery for ten dozen Bolivian orchids? Can we deliver to Molly Sherbin there?"

"Ah . . . sure. She's right here. Sharon, I mean Molly, someone is sending flowers. She said it's okay!"

"Okay, thank you."

"Why, Bella, you aren't sending Molly Sherbin flowers, are you?"

"Gee whiz, you figured it out. I am not sending flowers to Molly Sherbin or Sharon Jones!"

"Well, it's dinner time. See you later, Bella."

"Bye, Winston!" No doubt it's steak night again at the Beaumont's home! Speaking of dinner, I have to be there. We are having guests. And for a mere trifle of two million dollars.

Rene outdid himself. The people who sat around the table were Palm Beach's crème de la crème. The Von Oldorfs were there. Mr. Van Oldorf is some German Count. And the shipping magnate David O'Rourke and his wife, Bettina, were there. Bettina had fabulous diamonds on. Her designer dress by Vera Wang was magnificent. It was a simple black dress.

Bunny Davis, the chronicler of Palm Beach's comings and goings, was also there. You know you were in for a scoop whenever her white Rolls-Royce Coupe pulled up.

And, of course, there was Molly Sherbin wearing the same outfit and ring. It was all recently dry cleaned though. India never notices what other people wear, but she always notices what they say and what they do, which was clear when she introduced Molly.

"Molly Sherbin is new to me. She told me she is a cousin of the Sherbin family from New York. I know Cory Sherbin from my college days. Molly wants a two million dollar minimum donation from us for wayward boys in West Palm Beach. She will give a presentation on her program. No one is obligated to donate. But let's hear her out. Molly, the floor is yours."

Molly Sherbin, alias Sharon Jones, had a nice presentation. The cause is a good one, but you don't give money to a bad steward hoping for a good outcome.

"Molly that was very good. I am taking out my checkbook."

Not so fast! Time to jump into India's lap with the decoded message.

"Bella, do get down. Now! What's this Bella?"

India read the receipt and looked at the ring, granny's heirloom. The rich can be gullible, but they are not stupid or forgiving.

"Molly is leaving now. Please no checks anyone. More details to follow."

"India, what's wrong?" said Molly. "I thought you liked my project."

"Gino and DiMarco will show you out."

Molly Sherbin left and Bell-eye was on the case.

Bunny Davis and India were in council. If only my hearing were that good. Needless to say, Molly Sherbin, aka Sharon Jones, is now a guest in the state of Florida for other reasons.

The Boy's Game, a social club for wayward boys, is now funded and administered by the India Hays Charity Organization, called India's Trust.

Diamonds are a girl's best friend. And Bella is India's best friend.

Hey, Rene, what's for lunch? How about a little "Sherbin" after your meal?

THE END

MIDAS, YOU SHOULD BE COVERED IN GOLD

My name is Bella. I run a detective agency in Palm Beach, Florida. I have only one client, the fabulously rich heiress India Hays. I live near Vita Serena in an old Addison Mizner house built in the 20s. Hello to you, old flappers! I live next door to the Beaumonts. Winston Beaumont III is my assistant. With his good looks and my brains, we solve crimes against my heiress, India Hays.

Palm Beach is only fourteen miles long and three blocks wide, but I can assure you that under this tropical sun, intrigue never rests.

India is coming this way now. We are going shopping. There's Gino, DiMarco, and Marcus. I call them the three goons. Gino and DiMarco are rather mean. They look like US

Marines in suits. Very tough, and I mean really tough. Both are into martial arts, and both are licensed by the states of Florida and New York to carry concealed sidearms. Marcus has taken the state's driving course that covers how to handle robbery, terrorists, evasion, and kidnapping. He is also licensed to carry a sidearm. I'm repeating myself. Such is the world we live in. One never knows when one might have to protect oneself. Well, it's off to Worth Avenue today. I think we are going to 150 Worth Avenue, a beautiful Mediterranean revival-style shopping place. We are going to Saks Fifth Avenue. India loves Saks. You can find anything there. And then we are visiting Salvatore Ferragamos, the wonderful place for shoes and handbags. Oh, the Ferragamos. Such flair!

All of us are in the Bentley now. India is on the phone. Starvos Mykenos is coming to Palm Beach via his magnificent yacht, Alexander. She wants to invite him over for dinner. She needs some contributions for her social club for wayward boys, called The Boy's Game. India's Trust is always seeking volunteers and contributions for a good cause. Her current cause is helping young men develop a sense of self-worth and an enduring, tenacious work ethic. She wants to help them set goals and achieve them. Palm Beach is home to the working rich and the idle rich. India is the working rich. Her father expects her to have new ideas and new deals always going. She is also expected to share her wealth through India's Trust to help the less fortunate. India has to continuously increase her net worth. This doesn't mean owning stuff. She has to own things that produce an income and have value. Her money has to work for her. She likes real estate and new businesses that foster new, creative ideas. "Ideas move the world" is her motto.

She's wearing a silk chiffon party dress by Prada and Sigerson Morrison strappy sandals. She is also wearing Robert Lee Morris sterling silver bangles on both arms. Her perfume is Ralph Lauren's "Romance." She looks like a million dollars. Well, in this case, she looks like millions of dollars. I am a Chihuahua. You didn't know? My job, besides looking good, is to protect India from rogues, thieves, and poseurs. I work around the clock, 365 days a year.

Well, guess who we ran into? India is walking down the avenue and a very fashionable Chihuahua is by her side as she is about to be seated for lunch. That name is called and voilà, here we are.

"You are Paris Mykenos?" India appears startled.

"Yes I am. Starvos Mykenos is my uncle."

"You are so young and so handsome!"

"You don't hurt the eyes either, India."

"Well, I see that our two dogs have met. Your Yorkie is so cute. What's his name?"

"Aristotle. We call him Ari."

"Ari, come here!"

Now wait one minute! This is a one-dog, one-heiress town.

"Bella, are you jealous of Paris's Aristotle? I didn't call you."

Jealous? I am mad! A girl has to protect her turf in Palm Beach.

"India, may I call upon you later? I have my yacht, Alexander, here."

"I won't see your yacht tonight, but I will have dinner with you at the Breakers Hotel."

"You're on!"

Paris Mykenos and Aristotle Mykenos walked into our lives and now they were walking out.

"Bella, Aristotle and Paris left you a gift. It must be a doggy treat."

I didn't know about that! There's a box, Tiffany blue, with "Bella" written on it. Well, a girl never turns down Tiffany's.

"Open it later, Bella. It's time for lunch and I have to get ready for my date tonight. You are going too. Aristotle is so cute!"

Me and the Greek? I don't think so. He's so hairy. Not my type. The things girls must do together. We have to get our hair and nails done. And don't forget our massages. It's always a change of plans, but this is Palm Beach. India Hays Mykenos. How does that sound? I would be Bella Mykenos. No, no. I mustn't think too far ahead.

The venerable Breakers Hotel. There is also the wonderful Ritz-Carlton and equally beautiful Four Seasons hotel.

Paris Mykenos is quite a catch for any girl. But India is quite a catch also. Their money can change the world, like Bill and Melinda Gates. Powerful couples are always needed! Look at them dancing—Cole Porter, Ira Gershwin, and Noel Coward. All we need now is the late Bobby Short—too young and gone too soon!

And I have opened my gift. Ari Mykenos gave me a piece of beautiful Tiffany's silver. But inside was a cryptic note which reads, "You must meet me. I have convinced Paris to come to Palm Beach to meet your heiress so that I would meet you. Paris is in danger. I think his uncle, Starvos, is stealing from him. I need your urgent help."

Bell-eye is on the case again! You know what? I will take the case. It's worth it. There's always a crook somewhere!

"You're a lovely dancer, India!"

"As are you, Paris."

"What made you decide to come to Palm Beach?" India whispered.

"I saw your picture in magazines all over the villa. And suddenly I sensed this urge to see you."

"Oh, I bet Ari was chewing your magazines!!"

"In fact he was, except the ones with your pictures on the pages."

"Smart dog!"

"Yes, a very smart dog indeed!"

Well, here comes handsome himself. A diamond studded collar, of course. It looks like all of them are grade A's. Where's my jeweler's loupe?"

"Hello, Bella!"

"Hello yourself, Ari!"

"Have you read my note?"

"Well, Ari, what do you have to say? Thanks for the jewelry!"

"Bella, let's get down to the heart of the matter. Paris Mykenos is very rich. His father left him a fortune. His Uncle Starvos is mad and is stealing from Paris's estate. Money brings many strange things together!"

"Oh yes, I have heard it before, Ari!"

"I don't have any proof. None."

"Intuition? Accounting reports? Eyewitnesses? Receipts? Undercover videos? Lavish spending?"

"I came to Palm Beach to enlist your help, not to present a case!" Ari stated.

"True enough. You are engaging me to find out something which may or may not be true."

"Correct."

"Well, let's not ruin our evening. I will start tomorrow."

Winston Beaumont III is really gifted. I give him books all the time. I am giving him an art book today. The rich always have collections. The Beaumont Mansion is full of art work. Here comes the dashing Mr. Beaumont now.

"Hey, Bella, I am enjoying my language book."

"I know, Mr. Rosetta Stone!"

"What? Another book for me?"

"Sure, why not? The Beaumont's don't need more money!"

"It's an art book. Vincent Van Gogh. Oh, wow!"

"I knew you would enjoy it. By the way, I was with Ari Mykenos last night. He suspects

Starvos Mykenos is stealing from Paris Mykenos."

"That's terrible. Hey, Bella, look here. It's my favorite painter, Van Gogh. I love this portrait of Rene Chambier. It's his most famous painting and I just love it."

"I don't know much about Van Gogh. Where is this painting?"

"The book says it's in a private collection. Boy, if it ever comes up for auction or for sale, the Beaumonts will have it!"

"You really get passionate about your art, Winston Beaumont III!"

"All Beaumonts do, Bella."

"They certainly do. Bye, Winston!"

The life of the rich and famous. Sorting through our things! Where do I start with this case? Maybe there's a crime, maybe there isn't. Is there a crazy Yorkie in the middle of all of this? I don't know yet!

"Bella, tomorrow we have a party on the Alexander. It should be fun. I am having baked salmon with oil, rice, cumin, and mint. I need to watch my weight. You want some fish, Bella? I have to be beautiful for the party tomorrow. Whatever shall I wear?"

Let me see. Salmon is good for me. I will skip the rice.

The Alexander at 305 feet is a nice Yacht with a helicopter and a swimming pool.

The stateroom is decorated with antiques and French Impressionist paintings. Wait, I don't believe it! It's Rene Chambier. Wait until I tell Winston! There's Ari. He's not bad, but too hairy for me. Ah, there's Paris and India dancing the night away. Who knows where he got all this loot from, but he sure has put it to good use.

"India, you still know how to dance!" Paris smiled.

"I do. And the yacht is lovely!"

"Yes, all of the art and antiques were my father's. I can never sell it. I cherish his memory."

Well, looks like the Beaumonts will never get that painting. Money can buy a lot, but not everything, like friends or true love.

"Paris, Bella and I must say good night. Don't forget, tomorrow's dinner is at my house."

"I look forward to it. Good night."

The launch pulls away from the Alexander. It was another beautiful night. At the dock, the three goons meet us. The Bentley purrs to life and we were off to our humble mansion. India is very, very rich, but her life style is simple.

Paris's father has such beautiful taste. I hope Winston won't be too disappointed.

"Winston, wait until I tell you about last night!"

"No, Bella, wait until I tell you about last night!"

"What?"

"Bella, we are having a private auction. Our art consultant and art dealer are coming. We are privately bidding for Van Gogh's Rene Chambier!"

"That's impossible, Winston! I saw the Rene Chambier aboard the Alexander."

"Two paintings in the same place?"

"Or the same painting in another place!"

"Hmmmmm . . ."

"Well, I think I smell a rat, Winston! Here's my plan."

Paris Mykenos came to our house wearing Madras Bermudas, Navy Sperry Top-Siders, and a blue Lono Piana summer-weight cashmere! He's so handsome!

Ari is on the yacht awaiting my phone call. I have sent the art expert and forgery specialist to the yacht. If the team identifies a forgery aboard the Alexander and the real Rene Chambier at the Beaumonts, we have the culprit.

"Paris, aren't you the handsome one!"

"I have a small gift for you, India. We will open it after dinner if that's okay with you."

"Of course, I want you to be happy. You are a guest in my home. Rene has made his chicken asparagus stir-fry. And we have a good Sauvignon Blanc!"

Ah, young people in love. Well, it's auction time. Time for Bell-eye to go to work.

"India, Bella just took my gift for you!"

"What? She ran towards the pool!"

"Come on, Paris, I want my gift. Bella! Stop!"

Well, it's through the hedges and onto the lawn. I can see the Rene Chambier through the window and Mr. Starvos Mykenos himself. Here's a surprise for you! Ari already told me that the Rene Chambier aboard the yacht is a fake. The real Van Gogh is here as verified by several experts.

"India," said August Beaumont. "Do come in! Oh my, it's the young Paris Mykenos. You, too, are welcome in our home!"

"Uncle, what are you doing here? My Rene Chambier! What is it doing here?"

Needless to say, the Palm Beach Police were there also. Old Starvos was charged with possession of stolen property with the intention to sell it. This one will never make the papers.

The Mykenos estate will recover their paintings and I stopped a thief.

India's Trust is proud to announce a most generous donation from Paris Mykenos, the Greek shipping tycoon.

"Come to Greece with me, India!" begged Paris.

"I would love to, but it will have to be in December."

Another successful case for Bell-eye! Watch the jail van carrying Starvos go. I know, I know. Another Palm Beach case solved.

THE END

POLO—WHAT A BALL!

My name is Bella, and I run the smallest detective agency in Palm Beach, Florida. My only client is confidential. But because you asked, I will tell you that she is the young and beautiful India Hays, one of Palm Beach's most desirable bachelorettes.

I live in a seaside mansion with my client. My sole duties are to be pampered and to protect the assets of my heiress from rogue artists, poseurs, thrill seekers, and downright scoundrels. Ask any number of the state's guests for my credentials. One comes to mind rather quickly—Molly Sherbin. She is a guest of the Florida Department of Corrections, and I am sure she is thinking about us in Palm Beach.

India is required to give money away. You have to help others. To this end, India has set up the India's Trust. This fund is meant to help those less fortunate. She holds parties, seminars, polo matches, race car rallies, and galas to raise money for her charity.

A recent case involved her charity. I call it "The Case of the Fallen Angel." Oh, the culprit isn't doing time, but his brother knows that someone in the family is misbehaving. Have you heard of Argentina? It's lovely and very famous for its cowboys, beef, polo players, and the Peróns. Speaking of all fours, I am a Chihuahua named Bella. India is my owner and only client. I live in Palm Beach with her and her staff. Our neighbors are the Beaumonts. Yes, that venerable family of money. Winston Beaumont III is my assistant and head researcher. He never leaves home, but he has the world at his fingertips, or, in this case, his pawtips.

The case began quite innocently. India's Trust began a new fundraising campaign for the wayward boys of West Palm Beach. It was announced in one of the local society papers. "Today it has been announced that the Wayward Boy's Polo Match will precede the World Cup Match in Palm Beach, Florida."

It's rather nice to have a story about someone you know. "International players are expected. The British and Argentine Clubs will no doubt have a strong presence."

I could read on forever, but I don't wear reading glasses and my eyes are tired. I wonder what's for lunch?

India and I, along with the three goons, are off to meet the polo players for this year's match at the Breakers Hotel. Venerable, solid, and always excellent. India is wearing her thirty-one carat yellow diamond ring, a beautiful Tutti Fruti bracelet, and a Bulgari diamond necklace with a black Chanel dress. Her shoes, Ferragamo. Her bag is by Hermes. She looks like a million dollars. The jewelry alone is worth that. That's why the chauffeur and her two bodyguards are here. The three goons are to guard the heiress and her assets. Both bodyguards are wearing sidearms. Both bodyguards are marksmen.

We're in the lobby now. I can pick up bits of conversation. A little Spanish here and there. Too bad the Beaumont lad isn't here. He has such a way with languages thanks to a book I gave him.

India is meeting the players now. That one has a movie star look about him.

"Hello, India Hays, my name is Carlos Barrantes. I am from Buenos Aires." He kisses her hand.

"Buenos días, Señor Barrantes, and welcome to Palm Beach. I am looking forward to seeing you participate in the match."

"My pleasure. I am always at your service."

Well, what a charmer! And all these people are polo players? Where's the waiter? I need a drink. Perrier, of course.

The small talk goes on for what seems like hours. India's events are always fabulous. They always result in good endorsements for the winners.

Well it's time to say good night. The handsome Carlos Barrantes is saying good night to India. He could sell ice in the North Pole. Look, there's Ira Levine, India's head accountant. Ira Levine knows where every penny is and where it is going! I can hear Ira talking to John Evans, another one of India's accountants. Apparently, Carlos Barrantes has made some bills against the trust, about 50 thousand dollars. India didn't authorize any expenditures like that.

"Neither did you, John, or I," says Ira.

I will have to tell her and get her money back. Carlos Barrantes has to pay his own way. I am going to have to do some research on him myself. I am going straight to Mr. Beaumont to find out who this Barrantes guy is.

"Well, Winston, it seems the Barrantes don't pay their bills. Of course, I don't know anything about this Carlos Barrantes."

"Well, I brought you some Spanish language magazines from Argentina, Bella!"

The Beaumonts are rather resourceful with their time and money. Theirs is old money.

"I have a rather recent article on the Barrantes."

"No, I am only interested in Carlos Barrantes."

"Carlos Barrantes is a twin!" stated Winston.

"What?!"

"Carlos and Angel Barrantes are twins. Identical twins, in fact. Their mother, Rosa Barrantes, can't even tell them apart. She placed a tattoo of an angel on Angel's inner arm. That is the only way you can tell them apart."

"Winston, your Spanish is impeccable. I bet you learned that from the book I gave you," said Bella.

"Don't jest so much, Bella! Either Angel Barrantes or Carlos Barrantes is in our match. And he is charging things to India's name left and right. When she finds out, she is going to be one mad heiress!"

"Thank you for your work. Good night, Winston!"

The Beaumonts are rich, very rich. Every problem is a minor one. It is easy enough to get the police involved. But India's Trust doesn't need bad publicity. We are only in the papers for our births, marriages, and deaths. Maybe after a swim in the pool, a plan might come to me. But for now, it's off to bed. Couldn't Rosa Barrantes have thought of an easier way to identify her two boys?

Well, I haven't received any more reports from the accountants. They have discreetly notified other merchants, hotels, and restaurants that India's Trust is not paying for transactions beyond her charitable event's day. The purloined debts will remain. However, her trust will make a determined effort to collect from Señor Barrantes, whichever Barrantes it is!

Well, here come the three goons. It's off to the printer to check out brochures, tickets, and a leaflet explaining polo for the uninitiated.

We are in the Bentley again. But for the polo match, India will be in her Mercedes Landau or new Range Rover.

Winston Beaumont III is quite a horse lover. While I am out, I will buy a book on polo for him. The Beaumonts don't play polo, but I hear they are frequent sponsors at celebrity tournaments. A string of polo ponies costs a million dollars! A string is about eight horses. Most people can get by with four. That estimate does not include stabling, veterinarian costs, food, or traveling with your horses.

It's quite an expensive hobby. But as Molly Sherbin was fond of saying, "It's a mere trifle—two million dollars!" Molly is now a ward of the state of Florida.

Here's what I am thinking. India's Trust is putting on a celebrity match for her cause. Polo players from all over the world are here to play. The winning team will receive a cash prize and gifts from sponsors. Barrantes is a well-known player. However, he has fraudulently placed charges against the Trust.

My job is to unmask him, get refunds to the vendors he has cheated, and to maintain the reputation of India and India's Trust. The Barrantes men are so handsome. Each one looks like a model. I say "men" because something tells me that Angel Barrantes is no angel. Carlos Barrantes is very famous, but without a hint of scandal. We will see!

Rene outdid himself for breakfast. India is off to some meeting. And I am sauntering around with absolutely nothing to do. Well, that is not quite true. I need help in the Barrantes case!

"Good morning, Bella!"

"Good morning, Winston!"

"Bella, I have information for you. In the Buenos Aires newspaper, there's a story about a doctor who is taking care of a famous polo player. That player has had a recent arm injury. What do you think?"

"Oh, so what's the polo player's name?"

"I don't know," said Winston.

"Come on, you and I are going to make an international call to Buenos Aires." I gave Winston his lines and we made the call.

"Hello, doctor, I am Angel Barrantes. You treated my brother. I enjoyed the recent newspaper article. I think I am having a problem with my arm also. Can I make an appointment? I hear that you are the best."

"Yes, I just saw your brother today. What a wonderful man!"

"I'm sorry, I have a bad connection, doctor. I shall call you back!"

Well, it seems that we have a fallen angel on our hands. Next time I see him, he will have to remove his shirt. It's only for confirmation.

"Well, Winston, another job well done. Please translate or get me an English copy of that magazine from Argentina. India is going to have an interesting read."

The big match is tomorrow. We all park our cars on the lawn. Well, those who are given privileges to do so. It's fun. It is our version of tailgating, so to speak. India has bought a new Range Rover with all the accoutrements. Rene will be there with the obligatory picnic basket filled with sandwiches, petit fours, and champagne. Did I tell you that I love champagne?

The weather is lovely. And tomorrow, the weather shall be worthy of my queen, India. Oh, and that gorgeous Barrantes hunk will be there. So will his creditors. There are bills to be discreetly paid. I live in Palm Beach and he does not. India has a reputation to uphold. It's simply a matter of honor. Did I tell you about Paris and the case of the missing diamond necklace, which was later found sans the diamonds? Well, that was a case of honor. I shall return to our present case.

Polo is a very old game played on horseback. Each team's objective is to hit a small ball into the opposing team's goal. Although the game originated in Persia, it was the English who introduced polo to the west. And it was in England that the first rules for the western playing of polo were introduced. The Federation of International Polo now organizes World Cup Matches.

In Palm Beach in April, we have a World Cup event. However, the India Trust has organized a friendly match prior to this event. In July, we will attend the Windsor Park International event.

As I mentioned previously, polo is played on horseback. Each team has four players. Each round lasts about 7 minutes, which is called a chukker. There are six chukkers for each match. In between chukkers, there are breaks of five minutes each. It's during these breaks that riders may change horses. That is the basics. Oh, and the goal is scored when one team's ball goes through a goalpost. Then each team switches ends of the playing field. There's much more, but suffice it to say that one needs money, horses, and skill to play this game. See you on either side of the Center T. Let's play!

India is excited about the match. While India gets ready, a brown envelope with the translated Spanish articles has been placed on her bed, where she is sure to see it before today's events. Her accountant reports are also in that envelope.

We are driving up to the lawn now. Everyone who is anyone is here. Hi to you, love you too! Lots of this, lots of that. Blah, blah, blah!

Now it's time for polo. Carlos Barrantes—or should I say Angel Barrantes?—is on the team called El Diablo. The opposing team is called the Angels. Well, this match has reached biblical proportions! Each member of the winning team will receive gifts totaling 100 thousand dollars. Angel Barrantes, posing as his brother, is in the hole for fifty thousand dollars in charges. As Molly Sherbin would say, "A mere trifle."

The match goes on and on.

The Diablo team wins! Can you believe it?

Well, Angel, I have a bug that I am going to drop in your shirt. Here he comes.

"I have gifts and cash prizes from our kind sponsors. Will team El Diablo please step up?" says India.

Carlos Barrantes is walking towards the dais. Here I go. Beetles are so plentiful in South Florida. Crawl, baby, crawl!

"Something's crawling in my shirt. Pardon me!"

Carlos Barrantes begins to take his shirt off. What a nice physique he has! I see an angel tattoo. India sees it too!

"Señor Barrantes, may I speak with you privately for a moment?" India whispers.

I can just imagine what is being said. Here they come now.

"I am happy to announce that Carlos Barrantes is donating half of his winnings to the India Trust. Let's have a round of applause for Señor Barrantes!"

Well, let me tell you what really happened. I could hear the conversation with my own two ears. After all, I am a Chihuahua.

Angel Barrantes was unmasked. He was given the options of jail or pay the money back. He accepted the course of least resistance.

India gave him a kiss and invited him back as Angel Barrantes. He had to pay his own way, of course! He asked India how she knew who he was.

"Angel, let's just say that I have a guardian angel who sees all."

Well, let's just say I worked all the bugs out and that's how I knew.

THE END

PRINCE OR FROG? WILL THE REAL PRINCE HOP THIS WAY?

My name is Bella. I run a detective agency in Palm Beach, Florida. The fabulously rich heiress India Hays is my one and only client. India and I live together in an old Addison Mizner house. She attracts undesirables. Well, her bling does. With my four legs and engaging smile, I protect India from the grittier side of life.

Palm Beach is only fourteen miles long and three blocks wide, but I can assure you that, under this tropical sun, crime and intrigue never rest. Together with my trusted sidekick,

Winston Beaumont III, I have sent a few scoundrels packing. Some are now wards of the state of Florida Department of Correction. A girl can never do enough community work.

India has been in New York studying antiques. New York has everything! Besides, if you have antiques or art, one should know about her collections. India's jet should arrive late tonight. Her crew is pretty good. Jack is the pilot and Jeff is the copilot. Gino, her bodyguard, went to New York with her. Gino usually works with DiMarco and Marcus here in Palm Beach, but her plane only seats eight passengers. Hmm, so there was room for three more people. Well, I guess you never know who you might pick up in New York.

I once went to New York and picked up a flea. He was tough. The only thing that convinced that flea to leave was a beer at the local pub. He jumped off me and the next thing he was on was a Yorkie, and I was itch free.

Well, we are in the Bentley heading to the local aero dome. Notice I didn't say airport. Marcus is a great driver and DiMarco has a loaded sidearm under his coat.

India has just called and says she is bringing company. Well, we do live in a mansion and, at last count, not all the rooms had occupants.

India is arriving at Palm Beach International Airport. Her Bombardier Global 8000 is very nice. It has a 7,900 NM range at Mach 0.85. It's also very fuel efficient. India doesn't own a yacht yet, but she knows a couple of people that do. And besides, I want to see one special Yorkie who is frequently seen aboard the Alexander.

Here comes her plane now. Jack and Jeff are coming in awfully hard. Service and maintenance aren't cheap. Everyone wants a bonus, but if they are costing us money or incurring expenses, that's a no can do.

The plane is pulling up now. There's India. She is stepping off the plane now. She has a Hermes purse draped over her shoulder. Her Giorgio Armani jacket is to die for. As usual, she wore her Patek Philippe watch. It's the Ladies' Automatic Nautilus in steel. Her father gave it to her, but she always moves on her own time. The Bombadier 8000 is a beautiful jet. Its range and luxury are rivaled only by a few other jets. It's good to see the mistress of the house again. New York has been good to her. But the guests! Are they staying with us, or is she putting them up at the Breakers Hotel? Philippe de Bourbon isn't too bad, but a Bourbon from some extinct Shanghai branch is odd at best. I mean, where did she dig him up? At a dim sung dinner in

New York's Chinatown? None the less, he's gorgeous with a Hollywood smile. His body is lean. Not an ounce of fat on the one. But the other guest, well, he's so grocery-store ordinary. I suppose if you polish him up, he would look like a shiny penny. But who knows, he might be sterling silver under that tarnish.

We drove to the Breakers Hotel. Our guests departed, and we are headed home. India was silent for most of the way, but she suddenly turned around and asked, "What do you think about our guests?"

Gino replied, "Excuse me, Miss Hays, what do you mean? After all, the only opinion that matters in this car is yours! And whatever Bella may be thinking! Just be careful." He patted me on the head.

Employees of the rich. Ever so diplomatic. It wasn't his place to comment on those guests. Besides, Gino didn't bring home any stray kittens.

Well, we are home now. The house is fit for a queen, one who happens to be home now. And don't forget a princess, too! I am going to the fence for a conference with Winston. Yes, that member of Palm Beach's richest family.

"Hey, Winston, I had an odd afternoon. We just picked up Philippe de Bourbon, who is from Shanghi. I thought the Bourbons were all European stock."

"Odd indeed. European royalty is so full of nooks and crannies! But I shall look into it. Europe has changed so much."

Funny, I don't remember Winston going over to Europe. But with the Beaumonts' money, Winston may very well have entered England.

Well, it's time for a nap and an afternoon of television. India only lets me watch National Geographic shows. Anything else won't expand my mind. But when she is gone, DiMarco will change the channel to the TCM channel. He loves old movies. He must have been a 1930s matinee idol in his prior life. We are watching TV together. It's a family staff sort of thing. This movie is old, but it's good. It's about a guy who pretends to be royal in old Shanghai. He's pretending to be a Romanov, an émigré from Russia. DiMarco, a sucker for any love story, shouts, "He would never get away with that in Palm Beach!" Maybe yes, maybe no. Could a Bourbon be a Romanov, or a Romanov, a Bourbon? In France, Italy, or Spain perhaps. But Shanghai?

Carl was quiet. Philippe and India are playing tennis. Philippe is controlled, debonair, and ever the gentleman!

Carl didn't say much to Philippe. In fact, Carl doesn't speak to anyone very much. India asked Carl why he had taken the appraisal course at the auction house in New York, he grunted, "Merely wanted to see how others might collect their things." Sounded fine to me. India thought it strange. Philippe just yelled, "Who cares!" Spoken like a true aristocrat.

Carl didn't have many clothes, but Philippe had tons of Louis Vuitton luggage. He moved out of the hotel and is now a permanent fixture at our pool house. Carl only has a ring that looks tarnished. I looked at it one day and it looked to be in the shape of two birds holding a ball and a shield. Where did he get that? A dime store?

I am now in the backyard at my neighbor's fence.

"Hey, Winston, our new guest is a horse. Those Bourbons have huge appetites."

"Bella, I have been researching. There are no Bourbons in Shanghai, except bourbon whiskeys. Let me show you. Here's my definitive book on European Royalty."

The book fell and the page was opened to the two dumb birds.

"What is this, Winston?"

"Bella, what are you talking about?

"Well, Carl has this silly ring on. It's a bird holding a ball and another bird holding a shield."

"Bella, this is the crest of the Asturia Dynasty. That bird on the left is a Golden Eagle holding the orb of temporal justice. The other bird has the sword of justice and the shield of mercy. The Asturia Dynasty is the oldest in all of Europe. All the kings are named Karl. The Asturia Castles are full of treasures. The wealth of the dynasty is incalculable."

"Sort of like the Beaumont fortune?"

"No, Bella, the Beaumont assets are limited. The wealth of the Asturias is infinite!"

"What is the source of their wealth?"

"Trading in minerals, such as silver, gold, and, recently, uranium. Also, their dealings are shrouded in secrecy. The motto of the Asturia is, "I shall see things. And in seeing, I shall be!""

"When Carl was asked by India why he had taken the appraisal course in New York, he blurted out, 'I want to see things!'"

"Odd saying, but it is exactly how an Asturia would comment."

"Winston, how can I tell if he is an Asturian for sure?"

"The heir has a mark on the right heel. This mark is placed at birth to indicate that life is the

Achilles's heel of royalty. A royal person has everything in life, but is still mortal."

"Winston, could that really be Karl of Asturia? He is so simple! But to see is perhaps to know. Living a life of secrecy. Declaring nothing, but knowing all."

"Well, Bella, you better have a look at that heel. I will find some document or proof of the Asturia Dynasty. Why, the bluest royal in the world is a guest at your home!"

"The Chinese bourbon appears to be old, but is very new! Lots of fakes out of China these days."

"What do you mean, Bella?"

"Philippe is an impostor!"

"How will you let India know?"

"What does the orb stand for? Do the Beaumonts have something that only royalty would recognize? Help me, Winston, I am grasping at straws!"

"Bella, in fact, we do. The Bourbons married into the Asturia Dynasty in 1566. The bird on the right has a crown of fleur de lis. That's it. Any Asturia of worth would know that."

And any Bourbon of any worth would know that? It's like saying Marilyn Monroe was my ancestor. Who wouldn't know that?"

"We have a small, bronze replica of the crest on the Beaumont-Pere's desk. I shall bring it tomorrow. Time for dinner, Bella!"

Well, there goes my partner. Philippe you are good, but not good enough. Tomorrow we are going to appraise some art and then the real prince will say, "I am his royal highness!"

"Bella, what's all that stuff in your mouth?"

Philippe, Karl, and India have just sat down after dinner. Philippe looks magnificent. Karl is pensive. His face became light when I walked into the room.

"Bella, you naughty little dog, what is that covered with mud?" shrieked Philippe. "Oh, India, must you keep pets in the house?" he said, chuckling.

Strike two, poseur.

"India, this is extraordinary!" Carl shouted. "Look at this, Philippe!"

"Yes, I did! I wouldn't give you anything for it!"

India said, "Well, Carl, there's a card with a picture of you. It says, 'Karl the tenth, King of the Asturia.' Would you like to explain?"

"That's not me. It's my grandfather!" said Carl.

"You are an Asturian heir?" India asked incredulously.

"Yes, I am! This beautiful bronze ring is an Asturian relic. Karl the sixth was the product of a marriage between the Bourbons of France and an Asturia Prince. He became king for a short moment. Look at the fleur de lis crown!"

Philippe shrieked, "We are related?!"

"No, we are not. There are no Bourbons in Shanghai. You aren't a Bourbon. This dossier prepared by the Asturia government proves you are an impostor. Your real name is Philip Gonzales from San Antonio, Texas. You are a high school dropout and your rap sheet is extensive. There are current active charges against you!"

"Sit down now, Mr. Gonzales!" India commanded.

The three goons entered the room. Señor Gonzales sat down. A knock interrupted the silence.

"Ma'am, the police are here," Lucy said demurely.

"Lucy, please have them come in," India stated with a voice as hard and cold as steel.

Philip Gonzales was considered an important criminal catch. He had committed fraud all across America. Carl, Prince of Asturia, convinced the Beaumonts to part with that old bronze for a nice settlement. Everyone was amazed that India was keeping company with the Asturias! But they are not exactly party people, are they?

Well, it's another day in Palm Beach. Let's sit on the beach, throw out the old bourbon, and bring in the good bourbon on ice for the man over there.

Don't mess with me! Strike three, poseur. You're out!

THE END

ABOUT THE AUTHORS

I have had delightful travels for thirty-two years. I vacation every year in Florida. I love Palm Beach, Fort Lauderdale, and Miami. On my travels in Florida, I have met so many interesting people. I am amazed at what these people do for a living. They have the most interesting life stories. Being a doctor for over thirty years, I have become a fairly good interviewer. I have chosen to write stories from a composite of imagination blended with reality.

India is a young college student.

And Bella, she will never tell!

Printed in the United States
By Bookmasters